A TASTE OF HONEY

Kamala Outsmarts the Seven Thieves

Rebecca Sheir

Illustrations by Chaaya Prabhat

Storey Publishing

CIRCLE ROUND, EVERYONE

Think about the last time you accomplished something on your own.

It can be a wonderful feeling, right? Knowing you're strong and independent enough to get something done?

Working with others is fantastic, too, of course. But in the story you're about to read, we'll meet a woman who learns that self-reliance can be very sweet, indeed.

Versions of this folktale originally come from Pakistan and India, two countries in South Asia.

So sit back, get cozy, and Circle Round for *A Taste of Honey*!

Once upon a time, in a village in the countryside, there lived a woman who had the most delicious honey you've ever tasted. Her name was Kamala.

Kamala lived with her father and kept beehives in their tiny backyard.

Kamala collected honey from her hives to sell at the market. But business was slow, and before long she and Father were struggling to get by.

6

She knew she had to do something. So when she heard that the king's son was getting married and all the villagers were invited to the party, she got an idea.

The royal advisor bought some of my honey the other day, and word has it the king loved it! So I'll go to the reception and ask His Majesty for help.

After all, everyone knows it's bad luck to refuse a request at a wedding!

By the time Kamala reached the front of the
long line of people waiting to chat up the king,
His Excellency seemed tired and grumpy.

But Kamala didn't let that stop her.

Your Majesty, I'm the humble
beekeeper whose honey you enjoyed
so much. But sales are down, and
my father and I are in trouble.

CAN YOU HELP US?

The king glanced down the lengthy line and sighed.

Well, they say it's bad luck to refuse a request at a wedding . . .

I TELL YOU WHAT— I own some land at the edge of town that I have no use for. If you plant it, and sell the harvest, you may keep half of the gold coins you make.

Kamala was thrilled, and thanked the king.

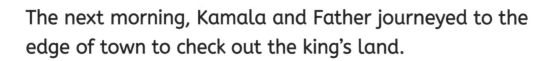

The next morning, Kamala and Father journeyed to the edge of town to check out the king's land.

Kamala had heard this desolate area attracted thieves and robbers, but she was so excited about her deal with the king that she had a smile on her face the whole trip . . .

. . . until she reached her destination.

OH NO!
This land is a mess of sticks and weeds and dirt! We'd need a team of horses to plow it, and we could never afford that!

Kamala furrowed her brow and tapped her chin as the wheels in her mind began to turn.

Hmmmmmm...

I tried relying on the king to solve my troubles, and obviously that wasn't the answer. I'll have to come up with something on my own.

Looking around, Kamala spotted two long sticks on the ground. Quick as a wink, she snatched up the sticks, handed one to Father, and told him to do *exactly as she did*.

Kamala made an anxious face.

Father did, too.

Kamala glanced nervously over her shoulder.

Father did, too.

Then Kamala began walking around the field, poking at the ground with her stick.

Father was confused, but he did, too.

Um, Kamala? Can you tell me what we're doing?

Trust me on this one, Father. I HAVE A PLAN!

Now, remember: Kamala had heard that thieves hung out around these parts. Sure enough, seven thieves were hiding in a thicket nearby.

And, just as Kamala hoped, her and her dad's odd behavior had caught the greedy swindlers' attention.

WHAT'S GOING ON OVER THERE?

Those people have been walking around that field FOR HOURS!

And poking the ground with those sticks!

The head thief sauntered over to Kamala and her dad. Though the rascal was burning with curiosity, he tried to act casual.

HEY THERE, FOLKS.
I hope you don't mind me asking, but what's with the sticks?

If I tell you what we're doing, do you promise not to tell a soul?

I promise.

Kamala glanced to the right and left, like she was checking to make sure nobody else was listening.

Well ... the king said we should plant this plot of land. Rumor has it there's gold in it!

We've been using these sticks to dig for treasure, but we have to head home now.

GOLD!

The leader of the thieves took Kamala's bait!

As soon as Kamala and
her father walked away, the excited
fellow rushed back to the thicket to
share the news. The seven thieves
immediately grabbed sticks and began
turning up every single inch of earth.

They dug all day but they didn't find
any gold—not one coin.

The next day, Kamala returned to the plot of land with a big bag of seeds.

Yesterday this place was a mess! Now it looks like it's been plowed seven times over.

HA!
Thank you, thieves!

Kamala began walking up and down the field, planting seeds in the earth. Suddenly, she heard a voice behind her.

The head thief knew Kamala was right, but he still gritted his teeth and clenched his fists as he and his crew stomped away.

This isn't the last you've heard from us! **THAT GOLD WILL BE OURS!**

Oh, you'll have your gold ... JUST NOT THE KIND YOU THINK!

All summer long, Kamala weeded and watered the king's land.

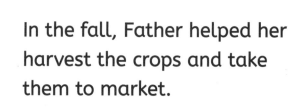

In the fall, Father helped her harvest the crops and take them to market.

The fruits and vegetables were so bountiful and beautiful, everyone wanted to buy them.

Kamala put half the gold coins into a bag for the king. She brought the other bag home and buried it under an apple tree in her front yard.

Kamala had a sneaking suspicion she had not seen the last of the seven thieves.

23

That night, as a full moon rose, Kamala glanced out her window. Sure enough, she spotted the seven thieves hiding in the bushes near the apple tree.

This was the moment she'd been waiting for. In an extra-loud voice, she called out to her father.

FATHER!
Can you believe how much **GOLD** we brought home today?

I've never seen so much **GOLD** in my life!

I hope you put it somewhere safe!

Don't worry! I hung the gold in a bag, high up in the branches of the apple tree.

Nobody will look for it there!

25

When it seemed that Kamala and Father had gone to sleep, the robbers tiptoed out from the bushes and peered up the apple tree.

The leader of the thieves jabbed his finger toward the top branches.

THERE'S THE BAG OF GOLD!
I'll climb up and bring it down.

The head thief really did think he saw a big, bulky bag of gold, so he shimmied up the tree trunk. But when he reached the very top . . .

. . . he discovered the bag was actually one of Kamala's beehives, dripping with golden honey!

Kamala's bees buzz-buzz-buzzed all over the thieves' not-so-fearless leader! He tried to slap the insects away, but he only smeared himself with golden honey. And down on the ground, the other thieves thought he was doing something else entirely.

Is he grabbing the gold?

And shoveling it into his pockets?

HEY!

IT SURE LOOKS LIKE IT!

He's stealing from us!

What a thief!

One by one they clambered to the top of the tree, intent on getting the gold. And one by one they were swarmed by Kamala's bees!

By the time the last thief got to the top, can you guess what happened?

The branch holding all seven thieves broke with a SNAP! And every one of them came tumbling down . . .

. . . along with the beehive.

Meanwhile, Kamala and her father weren't asleep at all. They had been wide awake the entire time.

Watching from the window, they weren't sure what was louder: the buzzing of the bees, or the hoots and hollers from the thieves as they stampeded away, dripping with gold.

Golden *honey*, that is!

Soon after her adventure with the thieves, Kamala's business took off. Turns out the grouchy king had recommended her sweet, golden honey to everyone he knew!

But even though Kamala was now prospering, the money isn't what made her feel rich.

She had learned the importance of using her smarts and relying on herself to solve problems. And that sweet lesson was worth all the gold in the world.

NOW IT'S YOUR TURN

Think about a time you relied on yourself and used your smarts to solve a problem. Perhaps you figured out a homework question all on your own. Or you fixed a broken toy.

Maybe you came up with a solution for a friend or family member who was struggling with something.

Whatever it was, grab some paper and something to draw with and make a picture of how you felt after you solved that problem.

What did you think of the trick Kamala played on the thieves?

Did you ever ask anyone for a favor and they helped you out, like the king did for Kamala?

Did anyone ever ask you for a favor and you helped them out? How did you feel?

What If . . .

Imagine if the king had said no to Kamala's request for help, and he didn't let her use the land.

What else could she have done to help herself and her father?

Think of an idea and invent a story where Kamala finds a different solution to get more people to buy her honey.

Will she have any troubles to overcome in your story?

Buzz Buzz Bee

Did you know that besides making honey, bees are important in the world because they help pollinate plants such as fruits, nuts, and vegetables?

Make up a story about clever bees that outwit a villain and do the important job of pollinating plants.

Make Some Noise!

Grab some instruments (if you have them) or things from your kitchen that can make sounds—for example, pots, pans, big spoons, or plastic bowls. As one person reads *A Taste of Honey* out loud, add in some sound effects!

What does digging in the field sound like?

What about coins of gold?

Or the bees?

Or climbing up an apple tree?

Hide the Gold

Are you as tricky as Kamala? She hid the gold in one spot but tricked the thieves to think it was in another. You and a friend can play hide-and-seek with your own treasure! Wrap up some goodies such as snacks or shells or little notes or drawings. Take turns hiding the treats. You can give one clue about where they are hidden if you want to.

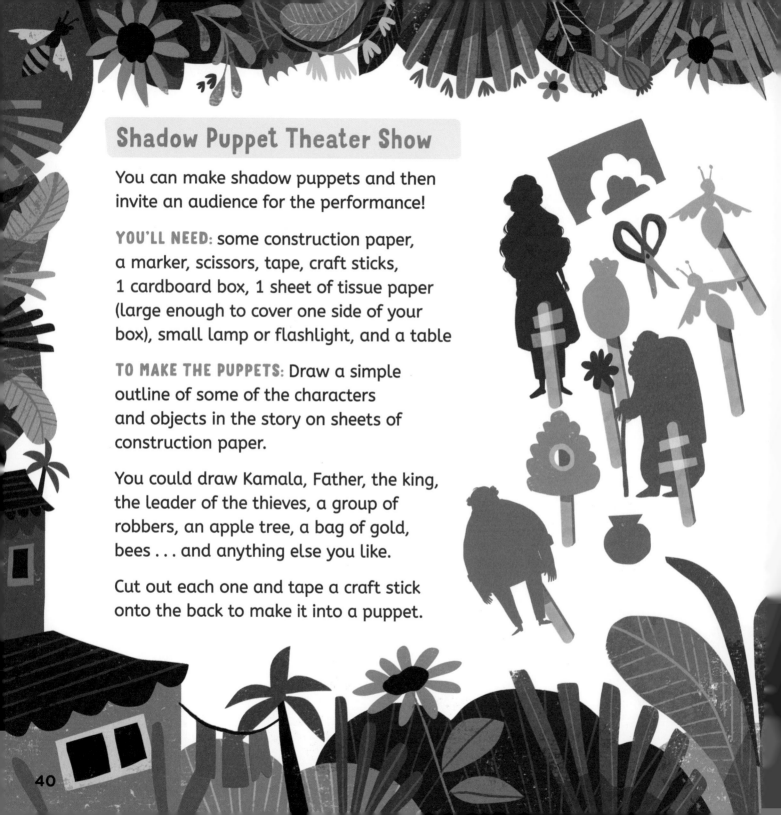

Shadow Puppet Theater Show

You can make shadow puppets and then invite an audience for the performance!

YOU'LL NEED: some construction paper, a marker, scissors, tape, craft sticks, 1 cardboard box, 1 sheet of tissue paper (large enough to cover one side of your box), small lamp or flashlight, and a table

TO MAKE THE PUPPETS: Draw a simple outline of some of the characters and objects in the story on sheets of construction paper.

You could draw Kamala, Father, the king, the leader of the thieves, a group of robbers, an apple tree, a bag of gold, bees . . . and anything else you like.

Cut out each one and tape a craft stick onto the back to make it into a puppet.

TO MAKE THE THEATER:

1. Cut out the bottom of a large box, leaving a 1-inch border around all the sides.

2. Tape a piece of tissue paper inside the box along the border.

3. Place the theater on a table. Put a lamp or flashlight in front of the open end, shining into the box.

4. Hold your puppets between the light and the box so they make shadows on the front of the paper. Now act out *A Taste of Honey*, and don't be afraid to change some things around and give the characters funny voices, too!

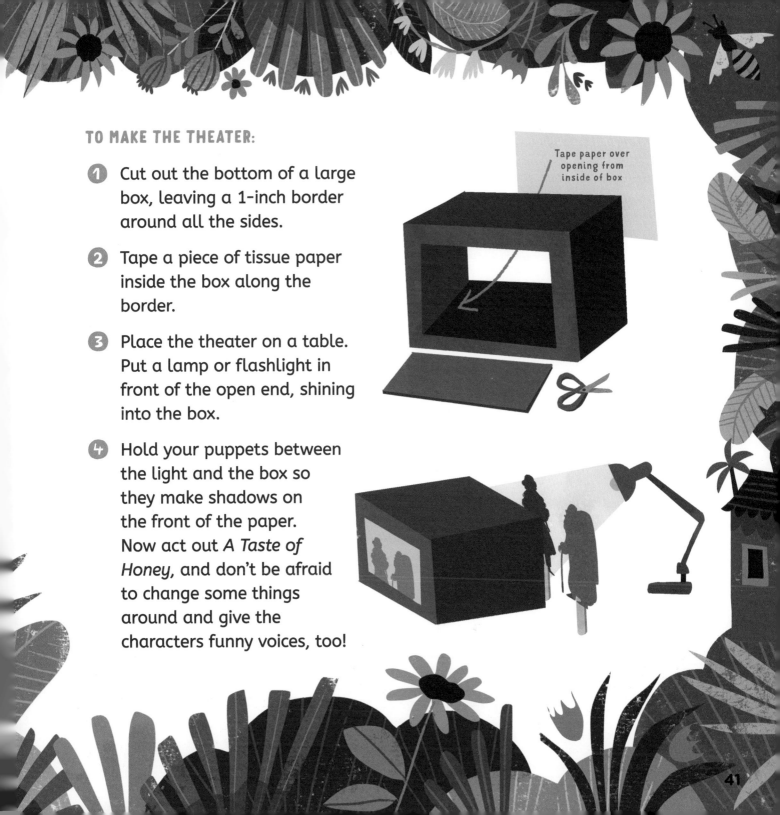

Tape paper over opening from inside of box

Run an Obstacle Course

Build your own obstacle course to thwart the thieves! Pull out some pillows, chairs, laundry baskets, boxes, sheets, toys, and anything else you've got around. Put them around the house or outside in the yard and plan a course that will be hard for the thieves to get through—but fun for you!

WINDOW

THIEF

THIEF PLAN

WHEN I CAME ACROSS THE ORIGINAL FOLKTALE VERSION of *A Taste of Honey*—often called Kamala and the Seven Thieves—I let out an audible cheer. After reading hundreds of folktales in which the woman or girl was a damsel in distress, a wicked stepmother, a nagging wife, or a fairy godmother, I was thrilled to find Kamala: a daring, spirited protagonist who created her own "happily ever after" by calling on her courage, imagination, and smarts.

In many of the original versions of the tale from India and Pakistan, Kamala has a husband—often a barber—who chooses to gossip in the village rather than work. In these versions, Kamala sends her good-for-nothing spouse to the king's banquet to ask a favor. When His Royal Majesty pulls a fast one and offers up a barren plot of land, Kamala comes up with her ingenious scheme. For the Circle Round adaptation, I chose to make Kamala the family breadwinner. That way, instead of trying to make up for someone else's shortcomings, she's trying to make her own dreams and aspirations come true!

Some of the original versions also feature a scene in which the thieves return to take revenge, and Kamala slices their noses with her husband's razor! This is a clever (if grisly) way to make use of Kamala's husband's occupation as a barber. By making Kamala a beekeeper, I opted for a different connection between her job and how she teaches the thieves a lesson—I hope in an equally fun and satisfying way.

Folktales are wonderful vehicles for helping us understand timeless lessons like persistence, determination, and creativity. In *A Taste of Honey*, the wise, witty heroine shows that anyone can have these traits regardless of wealth, social status, or gender. I hope you are as inspired by Kamala as I was!

—Rebecca Sheir

The mission of Storey Publishing is to serve our customers by
publishing practical information that encourages
personal independence in harmony with the environment.

Edited by Liz Bevilacqua
Art direction and book design by Jessica Armstrong
Text production by Liseann Karandisecky
Storytelling activities by Melissa Taylor, Imagination Soup © Storey Publishing, LLC
Illustrations by © Chaaya Prabhat

Text © 2022 by Rebecca Sheir
Based on the podcast *Circle Round*, produced by WBUR, Boston's NPR News Station

Storey books are available at special discounts when purchased in bulk for premiums and sales promotions
as well as for fund-raising or educational use. Special editions or book excerpts can also be created to speci-
fication. For details, please call 800-827-8673, or send an email to sales@storey.com.

Storey Publishing
210 MASS MoCA Way
North Adams, MA 01247
storey.com

Printed in China by R.R. Donnelley
10   9   8   7   6   5   4   3   2   1

Library of Congress Cataloging-in-Publication Data on file